SWINGING INTO HISTORY

TONI STONE: BIG-LEAGUE BASEBALL'S FIRST WOMAN PLAYER

Karen L. Swanson
Illustrated by Laura Freeman

CALKINS CREEK
AN IMPRINT OF ASTRA BOOKS FOR YOUNG READERS
New York

Marcenia "Tomboy" Stone loved baseball.

She didn't care that girls were not supposed to play boys' sports. Her dream of playing in the majors mattered more than the ache of not fitting in.

Someday, Negro League fans would chant her name: *Tomboy! Tomboy!*

Nothing could stop her from playing baseball.

Not even her parents, though they tried.

Mama insisted she twirl and glide, not just bat and slide. "Try figure skating."

Tomboy's heart's desire was a pair of cleats, not skates. But she knew not to ask. Her parents worked long hours at their Saint Paul, Minnesota, hair salon. It was the Great Depression and times were hard—doubly hard for a Black family living in a mostly white city.

Gliding solo was dull as ice, but Tomboy quickly won a citywide competition. She handed the trophy to Mama, snagged her mitt, and raced for the door.

But Mama . . .

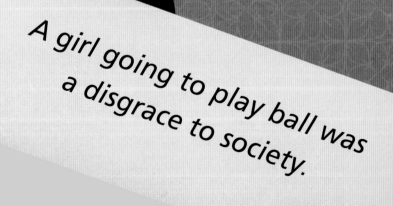

A girl going to play ball was a disgrace to society.

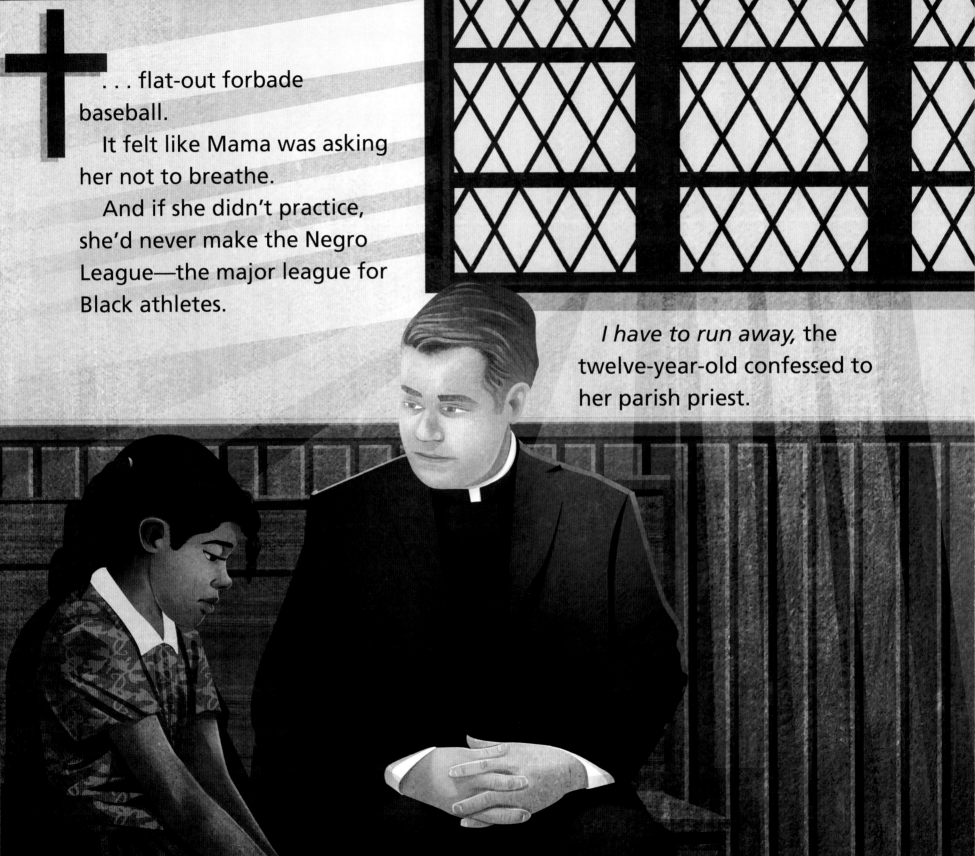

. . . flat-out forbade baseball.

It felt like Mama was asking her not to breathe.

And if she didn't practice, she'd never make the Negro League—the major league for Black athletes.

I have to run away, the twelve-year-old confessed to her parish priest.

But Father Keefe knew how to beat a squeeze play. He told her parents there was no sin in Tomboy playing ball . . . if she played on the church team.

I got a chance!

Tomboy hid her hair under her cap. She ROCKETED line drives

and KABOOMED homers, racking up wins.

Even so, boys hurled insults,
and the church coach
refused to teach a girl.

It made her want to
throw punches, but Tomboy
could not—would not—
lose the chance
to play.

She pretended the boys' insults didn't
hurt, and ". . . got a rule book and studied
it. I knew it more than the boys."
But you can't learn to turn a double play
just by reading.

Why can't they see me
as a ball player,
not a girl
who plays ball?

RULES OF
THE GAME OF
BASE BALL

RECORDS AND STATISTICS
Compiled by
PAUL A. RICKART.

When former major leaguer Gabby Street opened a summer baseball school, Tomboy's pulse raced. A professional coach would boost her skills way beyond books.

Trouble was, it was for white boys only.

As a Black girl, she had two strikes against her. But two is not three.

Gabby Street

Summer Baseball School

Learn to be a champ!

★ Lexington Park Stadium

And Tomboy knew
to battle when down
in the count.

I didn't concern myself that there weren't any women in the game.

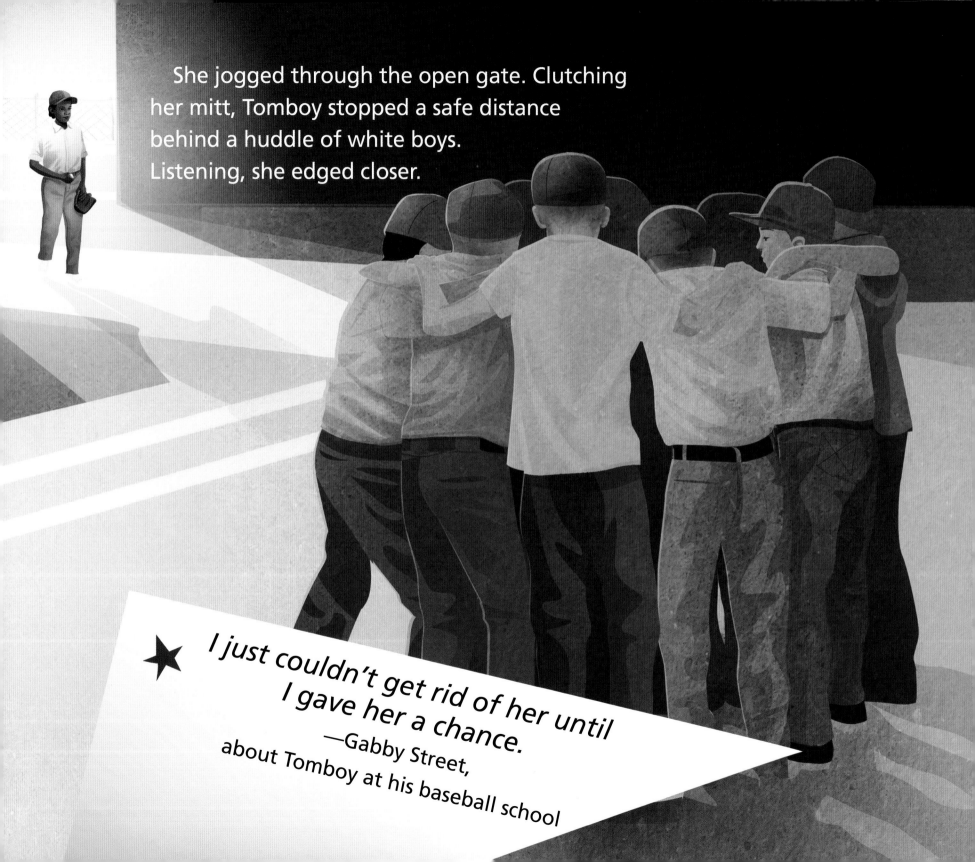

She jogged through the open gate. Clutching
her mitt, Tomboy stopped a safe distance
behind a huddle of white boys.
Listening, she edged closer.

★ I just couldn't get rid of her until
I gave her a chance.
—Gabby Street,
about Tomboy at his baseball school

Coach Street frowned and waved Tomboy away.

She rode off on her bike, then zipped right back.

Again, the coach waved her off.

Again, Tomboy rode away then circled back.

Until finally . . .

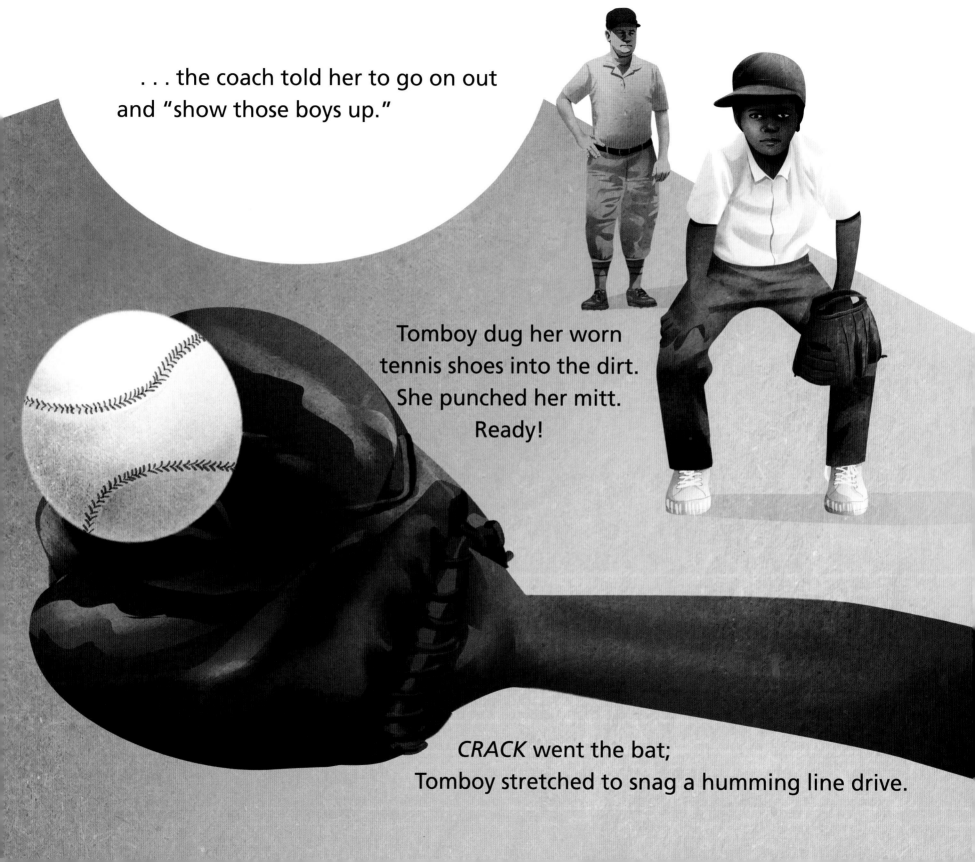

. . . the coach told her to go on out and "show those boys up."

Tomboy dug her worn tennis shoes into the dirt. She punched her mitt. Ready!

CRACK went the bat;
Tomboy stretched to snag a humming line drive.

THWACK; she neatly scooped a hard-hit grounder.

At the plate, Tomboy *BELTED* ground balls,

SMASHED line drives,

and *CRUSHED* long fly balls.
Going . . .
going . . .

The *Minnesota Spokesman* called her, one of the best young girl athletes in St. Paul.

. . . Gone! She'd gone yard!

All summer, Tomboy felt SEEN. She wasn't a girl who played ball; she was a *player worth coaching*. Drilling at second base, she wore the treads off her sneakers.

Could her dream of playing in the majors now come true?

Coach Street believed in her. For Tomboy's fifteenth birthday, he gave her cleats and the confidence to shoot for a barnstorming team: the first step to the Negro League.

Would they let her try out?

It was just like a miracle.

Tomboy asked to shag balls. From the outfield, her zippy, accurate throws home earned her a uniform. As for Mama, Tomboy "told her it was a way to make a little extra money."

The team of grown men who'd played semipro ball, "took her seriously because she produced [runs]." Tomboy hustled through high school then moved to California, changed her name to "Toni," and played in front of scouts recruiting for pro teams.

Miss Marcenia Stone, 16-year-old girl athlete, has been doing much to amuse the [Twin City Colored Giants] fans with her great catcher and wonder hitting power.
—Minneapolis Spokesman, July 31, 1937

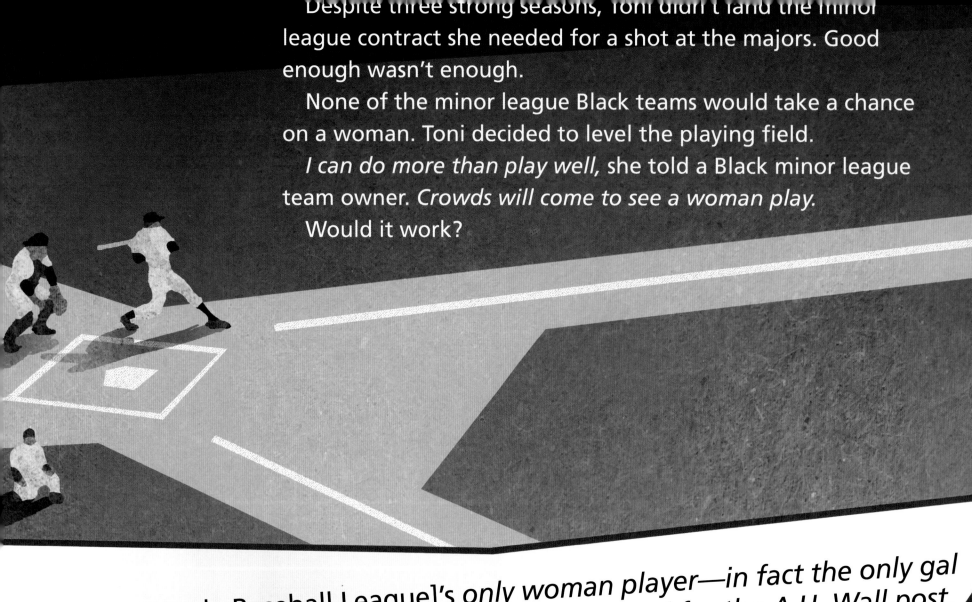

Despite three strong seasons, Toni didn't land the minor league contract she needed for a shot at the majors. Good enough wasn't enough.

None of the minor league Black teams would take a chance on a woman. Toni decided to level the playing field.

I can do more than play well, she told a Black minor league team owner. *Crowds will come to see a woman play.*

Would it work?

The [Peninsula Baseball League]'s *only woman player—in fact the only gal in bay area semi-pro ball . . . Miss Stone performed for the A.H. Wall post, American Legion, Juniors last year, and is an accomplished player.*
—San Mateo Times, June 21, 1948

Signed!

Toni was one swing from the majors!

The new starting second baseman stepped up to the rickety team bus: her ticket to stadiums packed with fans and major league scouts.

But her path to the Negro League proved harder than expected.

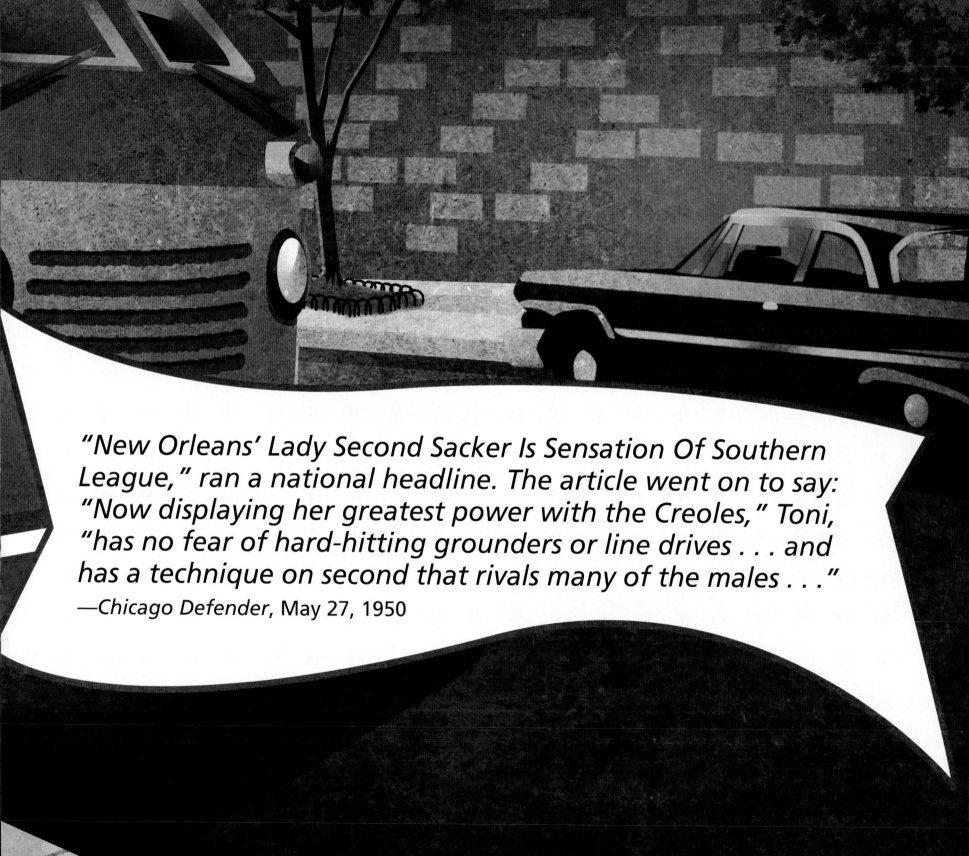

"New Orleans' Lady Second Sacker Is Sensation Of Southern League," ran a national headline. The article went on to say: "Now displaying her greatest power with the Creoles," Toni, "has no fear of hard-hitting grounders or line drives . . . and has a technique on second that rivals many of the males . . ."
—Chicago Defender, May 27, 1950

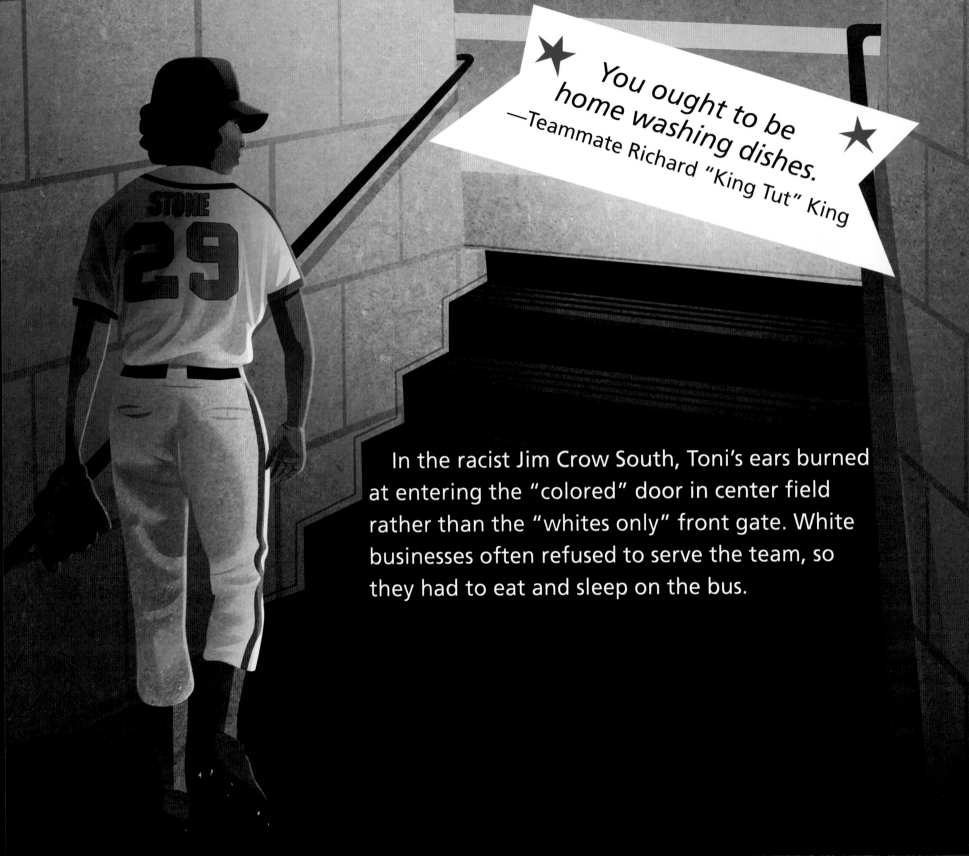

You ought to be home washing dishes.
—Teammate Richard "King Tut" King

In the racist Jim Crow South, Toni's ears burned at entering the "colored" door in center field rather than the "whites only" front gate. White businesses often refused to serve the team, so they had to eat and sleep on the bus.

Even in the home dugout, she wasn't welcome. To teammates she was "an intruder in a man's game."

That, at least, she could fix. To prove she belonged, she'd deliver runs.

Except she couldn't.

I gave them everything I got but they just wouldn't let me play.
—Toni Stone

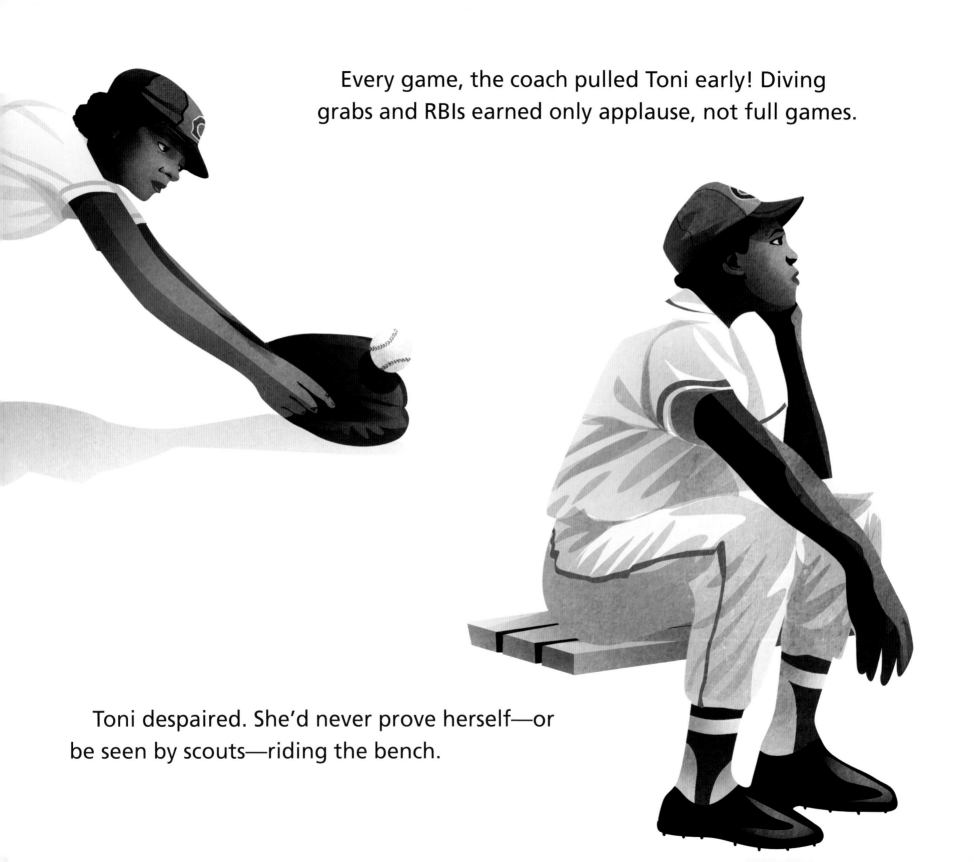

Every game, the coach pulled Toni early! Diving grabs and RBIs earned only applause, not full games.

Toni despaired. She'd never prove herself—or be seen by scouts—riding the bench.

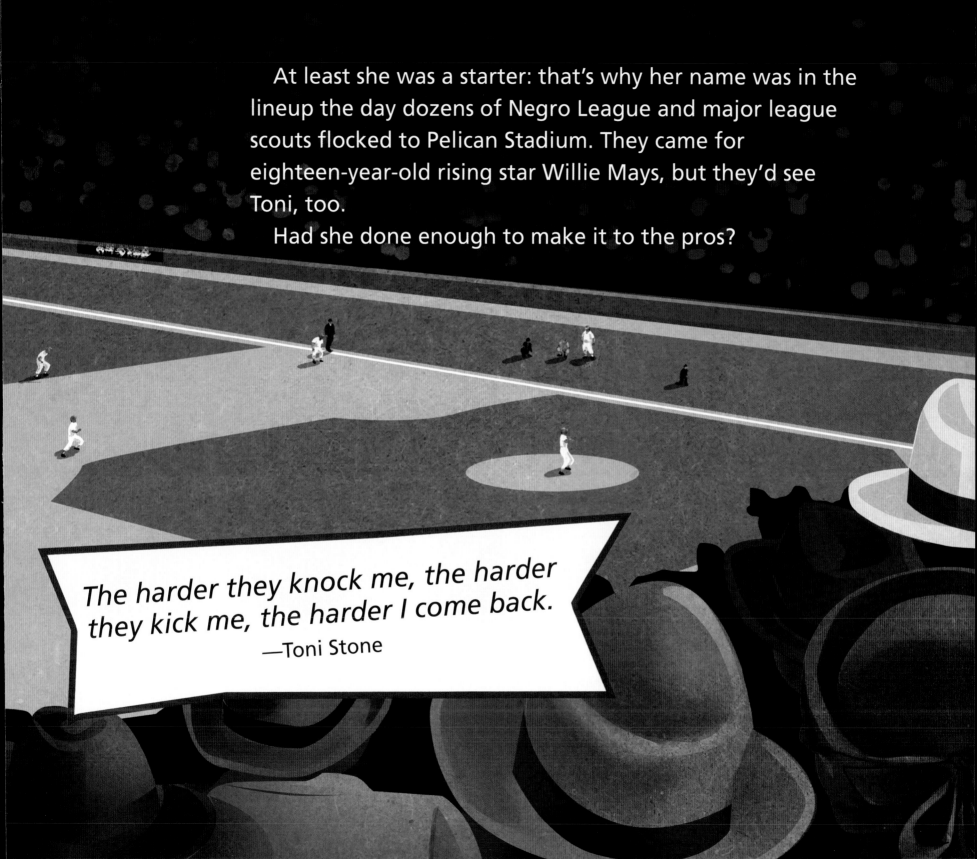

At least she was a starter: that's why her name was in the lineup the day dozens of Negro League and major league scouts flocked to Pelican Stadium. They came for eighteen-year-old rising star Willie Mays, but they'd see Toni, too.

Had she done enough to make it to the pros?

The harder they knock me, the harder they kick me, the harder I come back.
—Toni Stone

Yes!

When Hank Aaron was traded, Toni replaced him on the Indianapolis Clowns.

Newspaper headlines shouted, "Toni arrives!"

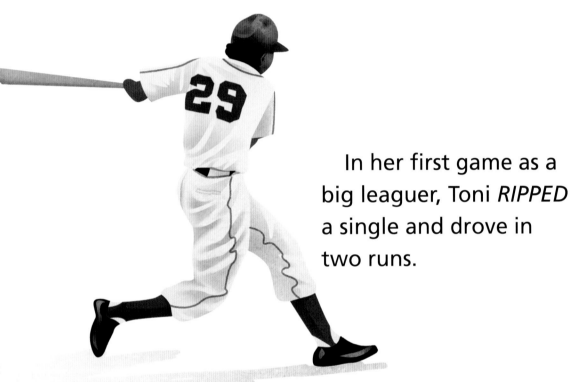

In her first game as a big leaguer, Toni *RIPPED* a single and drove in two runs.

One cleat on first base, Toni brushed dirt off her new favorite number and waved to the roaring crowd. Their cheers dissolved into a chant just for her: *"Toni! Toni!"*

Locking eyes with a little girl and her mama, Toni pressed her palms to her heart.
Then got ready to steal second.

I'll sum it this a way: Live a dream. Women got just as right living a dream as a boy. When the roll is called up yonder, I want to play baseball.
—Toni Stone

Toni Stone, first woman to crack the lineup of a Negro American League team . . .
—Pittsburgh Courier, April 25, 1953

AUTHOR'S NOTE

Wait, what? I turned up the speaker volume. It was June 2019, and people were talking about a new Off-Broadway play, *Toni Stone.* Immediately I called my best friend. "How is it possible that I didn't know a woman played professional baseball?"

I wish I'd known of Toni's triumph when I was a girl. I remember wondering why I had to toss a softball underhand when I could pitch a baseball as hard as any boy. Like Toni, I found softball slow. Unlike Toni, it didn't occur to me that I could play baseball.

Today, it's illegal under Title IX to deny girls baseball. Yet girls still have to fight to play. At the theatre I took notes; I wanted girls to know of the unstoppable Toni Stone.

Then I spent months researching. While I don't know for sure if fans cheered or Toni actually locked eyes with anyone during her first game, I made an educated guess. Toni drew cheering crowds all season long, and connecting with female fans meant a great deal to her. "I had women shake my hand from all over the country," she told reporter Bill Kruissink. "I'd see 'em and I was so glad that they touched me. I cried when they left."

Marcenia Lyle ("Toni") Stone was born on July 17, 1921, in Bluefield, West Virginia. When she was ten, her parents followed other family members to Saint Paul, Minnesota.

As a Black girl, Toni endured relentless racism. She faced gender discrimination every single day. It started early and it began at home. In the ESPN *Outside The Lines* feature about Toni, she said, "My folks didn't want me to play no sports, you know. Not no baseball. Sort of a disgrace, you know. But I didn't care."

It frustrated Toni that her gender mattered. Baseball is a game of statistics; if she pounded more homers or RBIs (runs batted in) than anyone else, why shouldn't she play? Indeed, Hall-of-Famer Hank Aaron once said, "There is no logical reason why girls shouldn't play baseball. . . . Baseball is not a game of strength."

As for talent, she had it. Toni batted near .300 in the minors, earning the headline "New Orleans' Lady Second Sacker Is Sensation of Southern League" in the *Chicago Defender*. "She was a very good baseball player," recalled Hammerin' Hank Aaron. Toni also competed against Hall-of-Famer Ernie Banks, who said: "She stood tall, didn't give up and was very determined. It was rugged for her, but she dealt with all her stuff. . . . She was so talented."

But from the playground to the pros, Toni's gender was an ever-present obstacle:

To get scouted, she needed to play American Legion ball, which was for boys under eighteen. She had to change her name (and lop ten years off her age).

When Toni learned the San Francisco Sea Lions were paying her less than her male teammates, she quit and signed with the New Orleans Creoles.

After replacing Hank Aaron with Toni Stone, Indianapolis Clowns owner Syd Pollock asked her to wear a skirt. She refused: "This is professional baseball."

Toni Stone was the first woman rostered in professional baseball for two reasons: her proven skill and that she'd be a ticket draw. Her minor league record mattered to

Indianapolis Clowns' owner Syd Pollock, who signed Toni: "It would do Black baseball no good to draw fans, then disappoint them."

And Toni did not disappoint. In the fifty official games Toni played for the Negro League 1953 Indianapolis Clowns, she batted a solid .243 and posted a .852 fielding percentage, all while playing only a few innings a game.

In no way was it easy.

Back when Toni played, there were two major leagues since the white major league clubs did not allow Black athletes to play. The Negro National League was founded by Rube Foster in 1920; a second division, the Negro American League, formed in 1937.

The game played in the two major leagues was the same, but conditions were not. In the south, racism was physically built into ballparks. At New Orleans's Pelican Stadium, a cage made of chicken wire corralled Black fans into seats in the blazing sun, separating them from white fans, who sat under a shaded roof.

On the field, Toni got called the same racist slurs as the male players, but also faced sexist insults from fans, teammates, and opposing players. If she made an error, it was proof she didn't belong. When she made a great play, humiliated teammates ignored or shunned her, telling her to "go home and fix [your] husband some biscuits."

After a successful season with the Clowns, Toni became the only woman to play on *two* Negro League teams when she was traded to the mighty Kansas City Monarchs. Like the Clowns, the Monarchs didn't give her the innings her play deserved, and that—along with the incessant racist and sexual harassment—took a toll.

Toni retired from the game she loved after her second professional season. Toni's career lit a path for two more women, Mamie "Peanut" Johnson and Connie Morgan, to play professionally with the Indianapolis Clowns.

Toni Stone

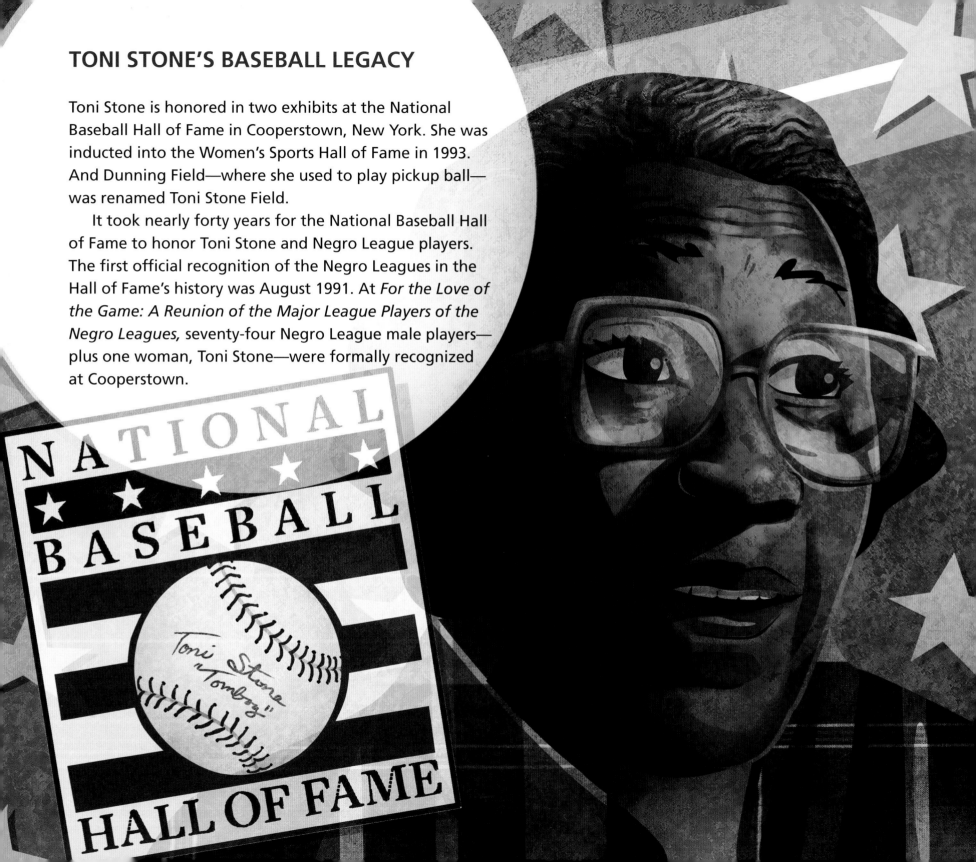

TONI STONE'S BASEBALL LEGACY

Toni Stone is honored in two exhibits at the National Baseball Hall of Fame in Cooperstown, New York. She was inducted into the Women's Sports Hall of Fame in 1993. And Dunning Field—where she used to play pickup ball—was renamed Toni Stone Field.

It took nearly forty years for the National Baseball Hall of Fame to honor Toni Stone and Negro League players. The first official recognition of the Negro Leagues in the Hall of Fame's history was August 1991. At *For the Love of the Game: A Reunion of the Major League Players of the Negro Leagues,* seventy-four Negro League male players—plus one woman, Toni Stone—were formally recognized at Cooperstown.

TONI STONE FIELD

MARSENIA ' TONI STONE ' ALBERGA 1921 – 1996
FIRST WOMAN TO PLAY PROFESSIONAL BASEBALL

DEDICATED SEPTEMBER 13, 1997

At the Cooperstown presentation, Toni spoke out, expressing gratitude for the official acknowledgment of her career as a professional ballplayer. Her voice cracked with emotion at finally being recognized. "I feel highly honored and thanks . . . to all of you guys for seeing I was here," she said.

After she retired from pro ball, Toni Stone returned to Oakland, California. She coached a local high school boys' baseball team and played recreational baseball through her midsixties. She died at age seventy-five in a nursing home in Alameda, California, on

TIMELINE

1920 *Feb. 13* Andrew "Rube" Foster and a group of Black baseball executives form the Negro National League. The Negro Southern League was founded by Thomas T. Wilson and a group of Black businessmen and baseball enthusiasts.

1921 *July 17* Marcenia Lyle Stone is born in Bluefield, West Virginia.

1929 Stock market crashes, starting the Great Depression.

1931 The Stone family moves to Saint Paul, Minnesota.

1930s Tomboy Stone plays with St. Peter Claver boys' baseball team and the HighLex girls' softball team.

1936 Tomboy convinces Gabby Street, former major league catcher and manager for the World Champion St. Louis Cardinals, to let her try out for his baseball school and earns a spot.
  Jesse Owens wins four Olympic gold medals.

1937 The Negro American League is formed.
  Tomboy joins the Twin City Colored Giants barnstorming team.

1939–1945 World War II.

1940s–1960s Jim Crow segregation laws in full force: Black Americans were prevented from eating in white establishments, sitting in front seats of buses, and much more; white supremacist Ku Klux Klan extremely active.

1943 Tomboy moves to Oakland, California, and changes her name to Toni Stone.

1946 Toni shaves ten years off her age to roster on an American Legion team.

1947 *Apr. 15* Jackie Robinson breaks MLB color barrier with the Brooklyn Dodgers.

1947–1948 Toni plays semiprofessional ball in the San Francisco Peninsula Baseball League (PBL) and on local teams.

1948 Negro National League folds; Negro American League continues.

1949 Toni signs as starting second baseman for the nationally traveling San Francisco Sea Lions. Upon learning she was paid less than her teammates, she quits and signs with the New Orleans Creoles.

1950 *Dec. 23* Toni marries Aurelious Alberga and sits out the 1951 baseball season at his request.

1951–1952 Toni applies to play professional softball in the (all-white) All-American Girls Professional Baseball League (AAGPBL) but never receives a reply.

1952 Hank Aaron signs with Negro American League team the Indianapolis Clowns.

1953 Hank Aaron traded to Major League Baseball team the [Milwaukee] Braves.
  Toni Stone signs with the Indianapolis Clowns, replacing Hank Aaron, making history as the first woman to play professional baseball.

1954 Dissatisfied with her playing time and a pay cut, Toni accepts a trade to the Kansas City Monarchs, becoming the only woman to play for two Negro League teams.
  Toni retires from professional baseball after her second professional season.
  May 17 *Brown v. Board of Education* finds racial segregation in schools unconstitutional.

1955 *Aug. 28* Emmett Till murdered at age 14 for allegedly flirting with a white woman.

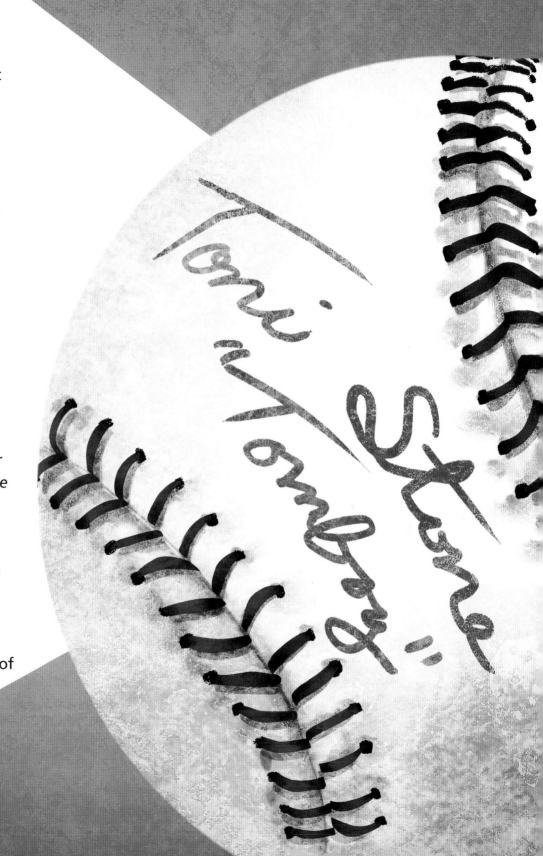

Dec. 1   Rosa Parks arrested for not giving up her seat to a white man on a Montgomery, Alabama, bus.

1960s   Toni begins coaching a boys' baseball team in Oakland and playing in local men's leagues.

1963   Negro American League folds.

1964   Civil Rights Act of 1964 passes, prohibiting discrimination on the basis of race, color, religion, sex or national origin; this legally ends Jim Crow segregation laws.

1968 *Apr. 4*   Dr. Martin Luther King Jr. is assassinated.

1972   Title IX civil rights law passes, prohibiting schools from discriminating on the basis of sex.

1984   Toni "retires" from playing and coaching local Oakland baseball teams at age 65.

1990 *Mar. 6*   Toni Stone Day is declared in Saint Paul, Minnesota.

1991   The National Baseball Hall of Fame formally recognizes the Negro Leagues for the first time at *For the Love of the Game: A Reunion of the Major League Players of the Negro Leagues*.

1993   Toni Stone inducted into Women's Sports Hall of Fame.

1996 *Nov. 2*   Toni Stone dies of heart failure at age 75 in a nursing home in Alameda, California.

1997   The city of Saint Paul renames Dunning Field— where Toni played pickup ball—Toni Stone Field.

2020   Major League Baseball officially designates seven of the 1920–1948 Negro Leagues as "Major League."

2021 *Feb. 9*   Toni Stone inducted into the Minnesota Sports Hall of Fame.

SELECTED BIBLIOGRAPHY

All quotations in this book can be found in the following sources marked with an asterisk (*).

*Ackmann, Martha. *Curveball: The Remarkable Story of Toni Stone, The First Woman to Play Professional Baseball in the Negro League*. Chicago: Lawrence Hill Books, 2010.

Afro-American. "No Gag, It Says Here. Clowns Report Signing Gal To Play Second Base." February 28, 1953.

Ardell, Jean Hastings. *Breaking into Baseball: Women and the National Pastime.* Carbondale: Southern Illinois University Press, 2005.

*Bartlow, Maria. Interview by the author, September 21, 2021.

Berlage, Gai Ingham. *Women in Baseball: The Forgotten History.* Westport, CT: Praeger Publishers, 1994.

Chicago Defender. "New Orleans' Lady Second Sacker Is Sensation Of Southern League." May 27, 1950.

Dare to Compete: The Struggle of Women in Sports (HBO documentary, Ross Greenberg, executive producer), 1999.

*Davis, Merlene. "Female Baseball Player Got the Ball Rolling." *Lexington Herald-Leader*, November 28, 1996, 74.

Ebony. "Lady Ball Player: Toni Stone Is First of Sex to Play With Professional Team." July 1953, 52.

*Egan, Erin. "Toni Stone Was One of the Only Women Ever to Play Pro Baseball With Men." *Sports Illustrated for Kids,* April 1994, vol. 6, issue 4, 26.

Grow, Doug. "She Wasn't Afraid to Swing for the Fences." *Minneapolis Star Tribune*, March 6, 1990.

Hall, Alvin. *The Cooperstown Symposium on Baseball and American Culture, 1997.* Edited by Peter M. Rutkoff. Jefferson, NC: McFarland & Company, 2000.

*Hayes, Bob. "To This Ms., Diamond Is Made of Dirt." *San Francisco Examiner*, May 4, 1976.

Heaphy, Leslie A. and Mel Anthony May. *Encyclopedia of Women and Baseball.* Jefferson, NC: McFarland & Company, 2006.

Heaphy, Leslie A. *The Negro Leagues: 1869–1960.* Jefferson, NC: McFarland & Company, 2003.

*"Honoring a Local Hero," *Minnesota Women's Press.* vol. 5, no. 25, March 14–27, 1990, 11.

Minneapolis Spokesman. "Popular School Girl Athlete Auto Victim." June 6, 1935.

*"OTL Toni Stone." Produced by Tina Cerbone and edited by Douglas Fitzsimmons. Vimeo, Uploaded by Douglas Fitzsimmons. February 2012. vimeo.com/39482919.

Peterson, Robert. *Only the Ball Was White: A History of Legendary Black Players and All-Black Professional Teams.* New York: Gramercy Books, 1999.

Pittsburgh Courier. "Toni Arrives." April 25, 1953.

*Pollock, Alan J. *Barnstorming to Heaven: Syd Pollock and His Great Black Teams.* Tuscaloosa: University of Alabama Press, 2006.

San Mateo (CA) Times. "Stars Shine for 6 Frames, Fade, Bow to Newells, 26-6." June 21, 1948.

*Stone, Toni. Interview by Bill Kruissink. March 27, 1996. National Baseball Hall of Fame and Museum, Inc. Cooperstown, New York.

*Thomas, Ron. "Baseball Pioneer Looks Back: Woman Played in Negro Leagues," *San Francisco Chronicle*, August 23, 1991.

"Toni Stone." Negro League Baseball Players Association website. nlbpa.com/the-athletes/stone-toni.

Toni Stone. Written by Lydia R. Diamond, directed by Pam MacKinnon, performance by April Mathis, Roundabout Theater Company, June 28, 2019, Laura Pels Theater, New York, NY.

*Uris, Dorothy. *Say It Again: Dorothy Uris' Personal Collection of Quotes, Comments, & Anecdotes.* New York: E. P. Dutton, 1979, 214.

Van Lueven, Holly. "Breaking the Gender Barrier in the Negro League," *Sports Illustrated,* October 13, 2020. si.com/mlb/2020/10/13/breaking-the-gender-barrier-in-the-negro-league.

Toni's strong arm in action.

ACKNOWLEDGMENTS

Martha Ackmann's impeccably researched, beautifully written biography of Toni Stone and playwright Lydia Diamond's moving Off-Broadway adaptation were my inspiration; their work enabled me to tell children about Toni's incredible achievement.

For their support and assistance, I am grateful to: Dr. Raymond Doswell, vice president and curator of the Negro Leagues Baseball Museum; John Horne, Roger Lansing, and Cassidy Lent at the National Baseball Hall of Fame and Museum; Dr. Leslie Heaphy, associate professor of history, Kent State University at Stark, author, and Society for American Baseball Research (SABR) vice president; Bill Kruissink, journalist; and Mikki Morrissette, publisher/editor of the Minnesota Women's Press.

I am especially thankful for the insight and support of Maria Bartlow, Toni Stone's niece. I'm also very grateful for the support of the entire Toni Stone family, including nieces Maria Bartlow and Monica D. Franks, and nephews Odin and Shawn Bartlow.

With gratitude to my indispensable critique group: Sari Bodi, Michaela MacColl, and Christine Pakkala. To my agent, Jen Nadol: I am immensely grateful for your positivity and insightful edits, always at lightning speed. Huge thanks to you and Jennifer Unter for championing me. And to Carolyn Yoder, thank you for shaping this story to be as fast-paced and compelling as Toni Stone herself.

PICTURE CREDITS

Courtesy of the Negro Leagues Baseball Museum, Inc.: 39, 40.

For Michael and Eric, always —*KLS*

For my Dad —*LF*

Calkins Creek
An imprint of Astra Books for Young Readers,
a division of Astra Publishing House
astrapublishinghouse.com
Printed in China

ISBN: 978-1-63592-813-6 (hc)
ISBN: 978-1-63592-814-3 (eBook)
Library of Congress Control Number: 2023918678

First edition

10 9 8 7 6 5 4 3 2 1

Design by Barbara Grzeslo • The text is set in Frutiger LT Std. • The illustrations
are done in Photoshop.

Toni instructs a young fan.